the Best friend BATTLE

LINDSAY EYRE

ILLUSTRATED BY
CHARLES SANTOSO

ARTHUR A. LEVINE BOOKS
AN IMPRINT OF SCHOLASTIC INC.

6|15

Library of Congress Cataloging-in-Publication Data

Eyre, Lindsay, author.
    The best friend battle / Lindsay Eyre. — First edition.
        pages cm. — (Sylvie Scruggs)
    Summary: Nine-year-old Sylvie Scruggs and Miranda Tan have been best friends their whole lives, but Georgie, a new boy in the neighborhood, could change that — and Sylvie will do just about anything to hold on to her friend.
    ISBN 978-0-545-62027-7 (hardcover : alk. paper) 1. Best friends — Juvenile fiction. 2. Friendship — Juvenile fiction. 3. Conduct of life — Juvenile fiction. 4. Interpersonal relations — Juvenile fiction. [1. Best friends — Fiction. 2. Friendship — Fiction. 3. Conduct of life — Fiction. 4. Interpersonal relations — Fiction] I. Santoso, Charles, illustrator. II. Title.
    PZ7.1.E97Be 2015
    813.6 — dc23
                                                                  2014024656

10 9 8 7 6 5 4 3 2 1   15 16 17 18 19
Printed in the U.S.A.   23
First edition, April 2015

For my mother, Ellen Bennion Stone,
and her infectious love of books

Chapter 1

It was eight o'clock in the morning, and I was standing on the pitcher's mound. Georgie Diaz was up to bat. He wiped his sweaty black hair off his forehead. He spat something gross right next to his shoe. He raised his bat into position. Then he smiled. "Let's see if you can get the ball over the plate, Scruggs."

I stamped my cleat into the pitcher's mound. "Oh yeah," I said. "Well, you'd better start closing your eyes now, the ball's gonna come so fast."

Georgie crouched lower, getting ready to hit. "I'll believe it when I see it."

"Throw the ball, Sylvie," my coach said in her exasperated tone, the one that means she is tired of being seven months pregnant and standing in the dugout, watching a bunch of nine-year-olds play baseball.

"Okay, Mom," I said.

"Go, Sylvie!" said my twin brothers, Tate and Cale. "Rip out his heart. Stamp on his gizzards. Eat his brains for lunch!" The twins were five, and they loved smack talk.

I straddled the pitcher's mound, my long brown hair tucked behind my ears. In one smooth motion, I pulled my legs together, the ball and glove coming up to my chest. There was a runner on first and a runner on third. I gave them both the eye. Then I looked into the stands where I knew my best friend, Miranda, would be watching.

And there she was, behind home plate like always. Her hands were clasped together; her face was tense. Her mouth opened. Her lips began to move. I waited for the thumbs-up and the "Go, Sylvie!" she always gives me when I need it.

"Go, Georgie!" she cried. "You can do it! Whack that ball! Home run! Home run!"

The ball fell from my hand onto the mound. I couldn't believe it.

"Come on, Scruggs," Georgie called. "Throw the ball already."

But I was still staring at Miranda, who was looking at me now. She gave me a thumbs-up and a "Go, Sylvie!" but it wasn't the same. What good is a "Go, Sylvie!" when you've just shouted "Go, Georgie!"? You can't cheer for two people at the same time. Not when those two people are enemies.

I picked up the ball and threw it at Georgie, but it was no use. My pitch went straight toward him, too slow, too easy. Georgie's bat hit the ball with a crack. The ball soared over my head and into the outfield, where it smacked into the fence and thumped to the ground.

My entire team groaned. Even my coach.

Georgie took off like a cheetah with short legs. He ran to first base, then to second, then to third, and then home, following the two runners before him. Then he did the stupid disco dance he always does whenever he scores. At the end of his dance, he pointed to himself and said, "Me? Home run? Oh, yeah, baby, home run."

I kicked at the air as hard as I could. That was not a true home run. The ball has to go over the fence to be a true home run. Everyone knows that, and I was about to shout this when my coach grabbed my arm.

"You're tired, honey," she said. "We got in really

late last night, and you didn't get much sleep on the plane. Let's let someone else pitch."

"Mom!" I cried. I couldn't leave the mound, because if I stopped pitching, Georgie would think he'd won. He'd think I was being kicked off the field because he got a hit off me. "No," I said. "I can't stop pitching now."

"Of course you can," my mom said, meaning she was going to make me.

I looked at Miranda. She was pushing her shiny dark hair out of her eyes and smiling at Georgie. "Nice hit!" she shouted.

Miranda, my best friend.

"Sylvie," my mom said. "It's time to go."

I stamped my foot into the mound. "It's still my turn," I said.

My mom crossed her angry arms and gave me her you'd-better-watch-it look.

"I'm not moving," I said.

"I'm the coach, Sylvie."

"No, you're not," I said, even though she was.

"Spank her bum!" the twins yelled at my mom. "Spank her bum! Spank her bum!" and it looked as if she just might. Especially when I kicked at the mound and a dirt cloud billowed up in her face.

But she didn't spank my bum. She just tossed me out of the game.

Chapter 2

Miranda and I had been friends since we were babies. We ate our first food together (something called "rice cereal" that should really be called "white-mush cereal"). We were in the same preschool class when Joe Kramer peed all over the "Meet at the Circle" carpet. In first grade, we built a fort made of cardboard, sugar cubes, and peanut butter all by ourselves, and they put a picture of it in the news. And last year, when the other girls started writing "secret admirer" notes and chasing the boys on the playground, Miranda and I made a club called "The Club for People Who Want to Do Fun Things." And Miranda has come to every single one of my base-ball games (except for seven).

She and I were meant to be best friends. We were made to be best friends. We had to be best friends.

We were such good friends, I didn't need any others. Miranda was the only friend I needed.

She was the only friend I had.

When she finally got home later that morning, I was waiting on her porch steps.

"Sylvie!" she cried when she popped out of her car, and I was suddenly in a colossal, friend-crushing hug. "Great game! How was your trip? Did you bring me back a surprise?"

I'd been gone for our regular two-week trip out West to see historical sites in the desert and go to family reunions. Miranda was a scientist, and she loved dead desert things like bugs and snakeskins. She stored her collection in a small toy castle she called her laboratory. I always brought her something back from my trips, something she wouldn't expect. Because Miranda loved surprises.

"I did bring you something," I said, and I held out a Baggie of shiny beetle bodies, a specimen I was sure she'd never seen before.

"Oh, click beetles!" she said, but when she reached for the bag, I didn't let go right away.

"Why did you cheer for Georgie?" I said.

Miranda pulled the bag from my hand. "What do you mean?"

I looked seriously at my friend. "Right as I was about to pitch to him, you told him to get a home run. And he did — except it wasn't a true home run — and we lost!"

Miranda had a shiny black beetle in her hand.

She was paying more attention to it than to me. "I just cheered for him a little. I cheered for you too. You can cheer for more than one person."

I frowned and crossed my arms. "Not in baseball."

Miranda began rearranging the beetle's antennae. "I know we didn't like Georgie before. But he's actually really nice."

"Georgie is not nice," I informed her. "One, he didn't invite me to his welcome-Georgie-to-the-neighborhood party even though I am clearly part of the neighborhood; two, he makes fun of me every time I pitch; three, he pretended he didn't know I lived in the neighborhood so he didn't have to invite me to his party; four —" I couldn't remember four. "Five, he's a boy, and the worst kind of boy. The kind who makes fun of girls whenever they play baseball."

Miranda was gently adjusting the beetle's wings. "He didn't mean to not invite you, Sylvie. His *abuela* made the invitations and she didn't know you lived here. She thought it was just the twins at your house."

"Ha!" I said, because Miranda had told me this before. After she went to Georgie's party and I did not. After I was the only kid in the neighborhood not there.

"Besides, that was three months ago," Miranda said in her patientest voice. "He's actually really considerate — he brought over brownies for the funeral."

I opened my mouth to say, "You didn't like him before. You used to think just like me." But then I realized what else she said. That there had been a funeral.

Someone had died.

Miranda put the beetle back in the bag. Her circle-shaped face went very, very long. "Muffin is dead."

"Oh no!" I said. "Muffin!" Muffin was Miranda's dog since before she was born, and he was really, really old. He was an awful dog, the absolute worst. He left pools of slobber in my shoes; he chewed up my favorite jaguar pencil; and he tooted about every five seconds, really stinky dog toots. Plus, he bit the mailman, Miranda's grandpa, and the neighbor's miniature pygmy goat. He'd been about to die any day now, and the neighborhood would be a safer place.

But he was Miranda's best pet, her only pet, and I knew how much she would miss him. "I'm really sorry," I said, giving her an I'm-really-sorry hug. "Muffin used to be alive," I said to comfort her. "And you really loved him because you're such a nice person. If he could have talked, he would have said, 'Thanks for taking such good care of me, Miranda. You always gave me belly rubs, even when I had those scabby bumps on my skin and my breath smelled like cucumbers.' "

Miranda sniffed. "You're right. He would have said that. He was such a good dog."

"He was," I said, though he really wasn't. But it was time to get back to the point. "What about Georgie? Why was he at the funeral?"

"Well," she said. "My mom invited his family over for root beer floats."

"Root beer floats?" I didn't even know her family ate root beer floats.

"Um-hmm," Miranda said, like this was no big deal. "They were really yummy. And when Georgie was over here, I told him about Muffin, and he thought we should have a funeral."

"A funeral!" I shook my head. "We can't have a funeral, Miranda. Not now. We'd need flowers and an organ and a religion guy and some veils to wear over our faces. And your birthday party is in two days. There's no time for a funeral."

"We already had it," she said.

I gasped. "You already had the birthday party?" This was impossible. I'd never missed any of Miranda's birthday parties except her third and seventh. And those were accidents.

"No, silly. Not the birthday party. The funeral."

"Oh," I said. "But you had the funeral without me?"

"Uh-huh. Georgie's grandmother played the banjo, and since Muffin's body had to stay at the vet's, we buried his collar and his leash and that thing he had to wear around his head when he had ear infections. Then Josh gave a speech."

"Josh?" I said. "Josh Stetson?" Josh Stetson was also a boy. He'd lived in the neighborhood forever, and he was really, really tall.

"Uh-huh. Then we dropped flowers and rice all over the grave and had more root beer floats."

Miranda took me into the backyard to see the tombstone. It was just old cardboard covered in splotchy gray paint. Someone had written on it in the kind of dumb handwriting all boys have that is small and impossible to read. It said:

Georgie's work for sure.

"Do you like it?" Miranda said.

"Huh," I said.

Miranda and I normally played together every single day. Normally, she missed me so much while I was on vacation, she couldn't wait till I got back again.

But this time, she'd had funerals while I was gone. This time she'd had Georgie. I wondered if she'd missed me at all.

"Have you made the bug decorations for your party yet?" I said. I said this to remind Miranda that I had helped her plan her party months and months and months ago and that we had decided on a bug theme together. Georgie probably didn't know about bug themes. Georgie probably didn't even know about bugs.

"I've made the rhinoceros beetles and the water striders," she said. "And Georgie and Josh are coming over later to help us make the rest."

"What?" I said as my stomach fell to the bottom of my feet. "They're coming over? To your house?"

"Um-hmm. They should be here soon."

"But why?" I said. I thought about Georgie's horrible tombstone, the one he made for Muffin. "You only need two people to make bugs," I told her. "And boys shouldn't make things. Ever. And I'm here."

Miranda smiled like the sun had just come out. "Come on, Sylvie." She bumped me with her shoulder. "It's not a big deal. It'll be fun."

I just stared at her. Of course it was a big deal. It was a huge deal. And it would not be fun.

I was about to say this when something occurred to me. Something very, very bad. "Did you invite Georgie to your birthday party?"

"Yes!" Miranda's wavy hair bounced. "Georgie hasn't been to a birthday party since he moved here. I invited Josh too. They're really excited."

I put my hand over my eyes, because this could not be true. She couldn't have done it. She couldn't! "But Miranda," I said, trying to stay calm. "It's a girls only birthday party. You can't invite boys to a girls only birthday party."

"It doesn't have to be girls only, Sylvie. It's not a rule." Then she started talking about how much I would like Georgie as soon as I got to know him. How we would be really good friends. How we had a lot in common.

This was not true. Except for baseball, I had nothing in common with Georgie. And we didn't even play the same kind of baseball. Georgie played mean, ha-ha, I'm-so-awesome-you-stink baseball. I played regular baseball. And I played it way better than him too.

As Miranda talked on and on, I scoured her yard for Georgie. He was like a flea waiting to pop out of the grass and bite me. He could be lurking in Miranda's bushes. He could be hiding behind that parked car in front of the Zhus' house. He could walk down the sidewalk any minute. He seemed to be everywhere all of a sudden, at baseball games, at funerals, at root-beer-float parties — maybe even at birthday parties.

If Georgie and Miranda became friends, Miranda wouldn't need me anymore. Georgie would bring Miranda beetles for her collection. Georgie would remind Miranda not to blow herself up when they played scientist. Georgie would plan all her birthday parties and help her do her chores early in the morning so they could go on a bike ride. They'd read books together, except Georgie probably didn't read books, and they'd build a city in Miranda's backyard, a giant city made of rocks — just like Miranda and I planned to do after all the birthday hoopla hoop was over.

"Let's go inside," I said. "Right now." And I took her hand and got her safely into the house as fast as I could.

Chapter 3

We were in Miranda's room, trying to find space for the new beetles in her castle/laboratory, when Mrs. Tan's voice came floating through the open window. "Miranda! Phone's for you! It's your aunt Ju calling to wish you an early happy birthday! Come get it outside, dear — I'm in the backyard spreading topsoil."

"Okay!" Miranda called. Then she looked at me. "Listen for the doorbell, okay? In case Georgie and Josh come over?"

"Um-hmm," I said, but I was too busy lining up beetles in the castle dungeon to really hear her. Almost too busy.

The doorbell rang one minute later. I rushed to Miranda's window, looked down at the front porch, and gasped in horror.

It was Georgie.

Faster than a cheetah, I raced from Miranda's room to the Tans' front door before he could ring the doorbell again. I opened the door, and there he was, still in his baseball clothes. Josh stood beside him.

"Hey, Scruggs," Georgie said.

Josh gave me a head nod and a smile.

I did not smile in return. It wasn't that I didn't like Josh. Except that he was ·a boy, Josh was all right as long as he was alone. But he wasn't here alone. He was here with Georgie.

"Good game today," Georgie said to me. "You threw a few decent pitches. Too bad you lost."

Georgie was always saying things like that. Things that almost sounded nice but really weren't. I made a you-are-so-not-funny face at him and pointed at the thing in his arms. "What is that?"

Georgie looked at the goldfish bowl pushing up against his stomach. "What does it look like?"

"A goldfish bowl," I said. "With two goldfish in it. But why are you carrying it around?"

"I'm giving them to Miranda," he said.

"Miranda?" I grabbed the door so I didn't fall over. "Why? For a birthday present?"

Georgie shrugged, because he always shrugs. "Yeah. And because Muffin died."

A terrible scene flashed before my eyes. Georgie giving Miranda the goldfish. Miranda clapping her hands with joy and inviting Georgie in and forgetting I was there.

"They're real," Josh said, pointing to the goldfish bowl.

Too real, I thought, glaring at the small orange creatures. "Miranda wouldn't want goldfish," I said. "Goldfish aren't good for anything — you can't take them out exploring. You can't do science experiments with goldfish."

"Science experiments?" Georgie said.

I rolled my eyes, because Georgie had no idea what science even was. "Miranda and I used to test things out on Muffin," I told him. "Like one time we wanted to see if he liked Christmas music better

than Fourth of July music and which one made him eat more Cheetos. Miranda and I do stuff like that. Together. Stuff you wouldn't like."

Georgie was staring at the goldfish. "Science experiments?" he said again.

"Yeah," I said. "With things like microscopes and beakers. Miranda would like the goldfish bowl better than the goldfish."

Georgie looked at Josh. "We could flush them down the toilet," he said. "Then we could just give her the bowl."

"No!" Josh said. He grabbed the bowl out of Georgie's hands. "That would kill them."

Georgie shrugged. "They'd be all right — they're goldfish. They can swim."

"Not in poop water," Josh said. "The poop would make them die."

"How do you know?" Georgie said. "Have you ever seen a goldfish die from poop water?"

"No," Josh said. "Have you ever seen a goldfish live in poop water?"

"I don't know," Georgie said. "Maybe."

It looked like this argument was going to take a while, so I stepped back into the house and slammed the door.

Miranda's mother came into the room. "Oh, hello, Sylvie."

"Hello, Mrs. Tan." I leaned back against the door. Georgie and Josh were not going to get in this house unless I had a dead body.

Mrs. Tan was drying her hands on a towel. "Did the doorbell ring a few minutes ago?"

"Yes," I said. "But they left."

"Who?"

"Nobody," I said as the doorbell rang again. "Oops," I said. "That was probably me. I think my elbow just rang the doorbell."

"Your elbow rang the doorbell from inside the house?" Mrs. Tan said.

I nodded and looked at her with enormous Disney princess eyes, the kind that make everybody start to sing. Then I silently begged her not to answer that door. *Please, please, please,* I told her in my mind.

But she pushed me aside anyway.

"Why, hello, Josh," Mrs. Tan said. "Would you like to come in?"

Georgie was not there anymore, and Josh — who was looking at his feet as they shuffled from side to side — said, "Um, no. No, thank you. I just wanted to say that the fish are both all right. And Georgie is going to take them back to the pet store. He says he's going to get something better for Miranda's birthday."

"Well!" Mrs. Tan said. "That's interesting."

"A better what?" I said. "A better pet?"

Josh nodded.

Oh no! I thought. "When is he going to the pet store?"

"Tomorrow morning," Josh said. Then he turned and ran down the front walk and down the Tans' driveway until he was gone.

"You know," Mrs. Tan said, "I'm glad summer will be over soon."

She wandered back into the kitchen, leaving me alone in the entryway. A dangly piece of hair was hanging in my face, making my nose itch, but I couldn't even move to push it away. I couldn't move at all. Georgie was going to get Miranda an even better pet.

Miranda walked into the room. "My aunt Ju just bought a live boa constrictor . . ." she began.

"I've got to go home," I told her.

"You do?" Miranda said. "But why? I thought we could get out the collection. There are a few things we haven't named, and I wanted to introduce the click beetles to the other specimens."

I looked at Miranda seriously. I grabbed the top of her arm. "We'll do all of that later. I promise. But I have something really important to do, something for your birthday. Something you will love. Just don't answer the door or go anywhere, and don't do anything without me."

Then I opened the door and ran across the street to my house before she could ask why.

Chapter 4

I called Josh's house as soon as I got home.

"Hello?" Josh said.

"Hello," I said briskly. I'd never called a boy before, and I thought I should probably be brisk. "This is Sylvie. I'm calling because you can't play with Miranda today."

"I can't?"

"And Georgie can't play with Miranda today either. Everyone's too busy to play."

"They are? Why?"

"Because Thursdays are busy days," I said. "So you and Georgie had both better stay home."

"Okay," Josh said, though he didn't sound so sure. "What are you doing today?"

"Things," I said. "Do you know what kind of pet Georgie is getting Miranda?"

"No. But I'm going to the pet store with him tomorrow. Do you want to come?"

"No!" I said. Okay, shouted. Georgie didn't even invite me to his party where there were billions of other kids. He'd never let me come to the pet store. "You?" he'd say right to my face. "No way."

"Oh," Josh said.

"Good-bye," I said briskly.

"Okay," he said. "I'll see you later."

Next, I called my dad at work.

"Can you take me to the pet store to get Miranda a pet?" I said.

"Yes," he said. "Sure — but wait! What did Mom say when you asked her?"

Shoot. I was hoping he'd forget to ask that question. Mom would never let me get a pet. Not for me and definitely not for someone else.

"Sylvie? Hello?"

"She's too busy to talk about it," I said. "'Cause she's pregnant."

"Maybe we should talk about this when I get home," Dad said.

"Never mind," I said, and I got off the phone superfast.

The trouble was, I'd already picked out a birthday present for Miranda — a make-your-own-candles-in-the-shapes-of-animals kit. If Georgie got Miranda something like a lizard, candles wouldn't be too bad, because a lizard was a ho-hum kind of pet. But what if he bought her a kitten, or even worse, a brand-new puppy?

Candles were nothing but blobs of wax compared to a puppy.

I had to find out what Georgie was getting for Miranda.

My alarm went off the next morning at seven o'clock a.m. time. The twins were still asleep, Dad was in the shower, and Mom was standing in the kitchen, stretching her pregnant feet.

"I'm going to go outside," I told her in an easy-going kind of voice. "To play and, you know, hang around."

She nodded as if she heard me, but wasn't paying any attention, which was exactly the kind of nod I was hoping for.

I grabbed a couple of muffins from the basket on the counter, put my binoculars around my neck, then snuck down the street to Georgie's.

Georgie's house is four houses down from my house on the opposite side of the street, and the good thing about it is the bushes. There are lots and lots of bushes around Georgie's house, which means lots of places to hide. I chose an especially thick clump right next to his driveway.

The bushes needed to be thick. Georgie's neighbor has a very scary dog named Dagger, who is only kept in his yard by an invisible electric fence, as if those count. Dagger didn't seem to be outside right now, but if he saw me, his name would come true, and I would have to be buried next to Muffin.

Nothing was happening at Georgie's. The garage door was not raising and the front door was not opening, so I laid on my back behind the bushes. If Dagger did escape, and he ran into Georgie's yard, and he found me hiding in the bushes, and he got me, I knew what Georgie would write on my tombstone.

SYLVIE SCRUGGS
SO DUMB
—
NOW DEAD

I yanked a leaf off the bush and tore it into little pieces. Miranda and I were different than most people. We didn't want to dress tiny dolls in rubber clothes, or feed stuffed animals on the Internet like Savannah and Rita and Haley and those other girls at our school. We liked to draw dragons. Or play croquet with hard-boiled eggs, or dig trenches and fill them with baking powder and vinegar just to watch them explode. Georgie would never do any of those things. Georgie probably just watched TV or played video games when he wasn't playing baseball.

Why would Miranda want to do that? What was wrong with what we did together?

I was waiting for red ants to come and eat me and end my horrible thoughts when I heard the sound of the garage door opening and a car engine starting.

I got out my binoculars and peered through the leaves of the bushes. Georgie and Georgie's dad were in the car. Plus Josh, who must have slept over.

Hurry, I told them in my mind. *Hurry to the pet store and hurry back, and when you return, say really loudly what pet you bought Miranda.*

They did not hurry. They were gone for over two hours. When Georgie's dad's green station wagon finally pulled back into the driveway, I was nearly dead of heartstroke. But I brought my binoculars back into position just in time.

Josh got out first, with a heavy-looking bag hanging over his arm, probably full of pet food. Georgie hopped out next, holding a small, brown, unmarked container. Georgie's dad got out last. His arms were empty.

Hooray! I thought. A boring lizard for sure!

But then the dad walked around to the trunk, opened it, reached inside, and pulled out an enormous box, and when I say enormous, I mean huge. Much bigger than a goldfish bowl. A leopard-sized box.

I listened with all the strength I had in my ears.

"Thanks, Dad," Georgie said.

"Take them straight to your room," Georgie's dad said.

"Them?" I whispered as they went inside the house. Them was bad. Really bad. Them meant more than one. In that box could be two monstrous rabbits. Or four not-so-monstrous rabbits. Or there could be twenty regular-sized rabbits, stacked on top of one another.

I don't like spying. I only do it when I have to. When I have no other choice. When the ox is in the mire, like my dad says, because oxes are supposed to be in barns, not mires, so sometimes you have to rescue them. Sometimes you have no choice.

I didn't know what Georgie had gotten for Miranda. I had to spy on him. I had no choice.

So I waited. I waited until I was certain he had taken the pets to his room. Then I waited a little bit longer. Then I waited a little bit more longer. Then I told myself if I was going to spy, I was just going to have to do it, and if I didn't do it now, I wouldn't do it at all.

With a tiny sigh, I got to my feet and snuck as sneakily as I could into Georgie's backyard. Georgie's house is long and flat, all on one level. It has six windows in the back like cars on a train. Spotting Georgie's window was no problem. There was only one curtain with bats and baseballs on the fabric.

An extra-large metal bucket sat on the grass near the house. I lifted it up and dragged it through some bushes until it was right beneath Georgie's window. Then I climbed on top and pressed my face to the glass, but it was no good. I couldn't see a thing. I pushed my face harder against the window, rolling my head left and right. But still, I couldn't see.

When I pushed on the side of Georgie's window, I did not expect it to open. But it did. It slid over so easily, I could have moved it with my pinkie finger. I could have moved it with my pinkie toe.

The room did not smell good. The floor was covered with shirts and shorts and underwear, yuck, and who knows what else. Probably mushrooms. But I couldn't see any pets.

Then I noticed something in the right-hand corner, closest to the window. It was brown on the bottom and brown on the top with glass in the middle. Like a tank.

I leaned forward through the window as much as I could. What sorts of animals did people keep in tanks besides fish? Snakes? Turtles? Not leopards, thank goodness.

What if Georgie had gotten Miranda a couple of sea turtles?

With shaking arms, I climbed through Georgie's window. I would be swift, I told myself. I'd look at the tank and hop back out.

I dropped to the floor, looked at the tank, and fell to my knees with a gasp.

Ferrets. Georgie had gotten Miranda two ferrets.

Hunched over so I could see into the tank, I watched the two ferrets running around. One was dark with raccoonish eyes, and the other was white,

like a cloud. Chewed-up paper lined the bottom of the tank, and there was a bowl for water and a bowl for food.

Ferrets are really expensive pets. I know this because my dad took me to the pet store once, and I asked if I could touch the ferrets. The pet store worker wouldn't let me, because ferrets cost one hundred dollars. "You can't pet one unless you're buying one," he said.

Miranda loved the ferrets at the pet store too.

"I got these for you," Georgie would say to her. He'd be standing at her front door with his baseball uniform on.

She would squeal and give him a hug. "Thank you, Georgie," she would say. "These are the best pets ever. This is the best present I've ever gotten. Sylvie's presents aren't nearly as good as this. Let's be best friends forever."

I rested my forehead against the glass. The white ferret pushed her whiskers and nose up against the glass to see me. She was clearly a girl. I named her Elizabeth in my head. The other ferret was probably a boy ferret. Those raccoony eyes looked like trouble. I decided to name him Albert.

I wanted so much to touch a real, live ferret just once, just for a minute. The house was quiet. Nobody was coming. The wire mesh on top of the tank came off easily. But when I twisted away to set it on the floor, Elizabeth, the white ferret, seized her chance and leaped from the cage. I turned back in time to see her tearing toward Georgie's bed.

Sliding into bases is one of my baseball specialties, so I dove on my stomach to catch Elizabeth. Like I do when I'm trying to steal third. My hands caught her around the middle. Her fur was slippery, and I nearly lost hold of her, but I finally managed to pull her into my arms.

As I was hurrying back to the tank with Elizabeth, the raccoony ferret, Albert, leaped from the cage like a cheetah.

"Shoot!" I said. I made a grab for Albert, but Elizabeth squirmed so much, I needed both hands to hang on to her.

Elizabeth slipped into the tank, no problem, and I put the mesh thing back on top. But when I turned back to catch Albert, he was gone. Hidden in the mess of Georgie's room.

Clothes and papers got in my way as I crawled around the floor.

"Albert!" I said very, very softly. "Oh, Albert! Come out, come out, wherever you are!"

Albert did not come out. Albert did not move.

"I can see you," I told him, even though I couldn't. "So you might as well just come here."

Oh, please, don't be hiding under Georgie's bed, I thought.

Suddenly, without warning, Albert tore out from beneath a clothes pile and jumped at my nose. I screamed, but Albert didn't try to eat me. He just landed in front of me with a "Let's play!" look on his ferret face.

Footsteps sounded in the hall. Albert froze, still as an icicle.

"Jorge?" came a voice from the hallway. "Jorge? Are you all right?"

I clamped my hand over my mouth so I wouldn't scream again. It was Georgie's grandma. She grew up in Guatemala and she always called him "Jorge." She was a big woman who I thought seemed really nice, even though she was related to Georgie. But she didn't sound nice now. She sounded mad.

I grabbed frozen Albert and ran for the window. Without even a grunt, I climbed over the windowsill, stepped onto the bucket, and crouched on the ground.

"It's all right," I whispered to Albert, who was quivering in my hands. "As soon as she leaves, I'll put you back in Georgie's room and shut the window so you can't get out." His little face looked up at me. His nose trembled. I patted his long, skinny back so he wouldn't be so nervous. "I didn't mean to take you," I told him. "The grandma was coming and I couldn't think."

His whiskers twitched.

"Well, I didn't," I said.

"*¡Ah, este hijo!*" It was Georgie's grandma. She sounded close, like she was by the window. "This boy's room. *¡Mira!* And he's supposed to tell me when he leaves." She sighed a tired sigh. "If I had a nickel for every time I've had to shut and lock this window, I'd be rich. *¡Cuándo aprenderá!*"

There was a slam and a click above me. The kind of click that means something is now locked.

I looked down at Albert. He looked up at me. "What am I going to do?" I said.

Chapter 5

I had no choice but to sneak back home with Albert. Georgie's grandma had said he had gone somewhere, and I wasn't going to walk around to the front of the house, ring the doorbell, and say, "Oops. I might have accidentally taken this ferret out of Georgie's room. Here you go." And I couldn't just leave Albert outside for Dagger to eat him.

Sneaking back home was much scarier than sneaking over to Georgie's. First, I had to hide Albert underneath my shirt with his nose poking through the neck so he could breathe. Then I had to tiptoe across the street like nothing big was going on. Then I had to walk all the way down to my house without attracting attention.

I was almost to my front porch when I heard two words of doom: "Hey, Scruggs!" I paused on the grass, one foot on a sprinkler head, both hands on Albert. It was Georgie.

"You should go over to Miranda's," he called.

Without turning my body, I looked over my shoulder and said, "Why?"

"To see the gerbils I got her at the pet store."

"Gerbils?" I whispered. What did he mean, gerbils? He couldn't mean gerbils! I could not move a

muscle. I couldn't even blink an eyelid. "Gerbils?" I said so he could hear me.

"Gerbils," Georgie said, emphasizing the "s." "Four of them. You can do science experiments with gerbils."

"Really good ones," Josh said.

"Don't you mean ferrets?" I said, gripping Albert tighter.

"Ferrets?" Georgie said. "Nah, I have ferrets. Ferrets are awesome, but they cost too much money to give for a present, so I got her gerbils."

"Gerbils," I said to myself. Georgie hadn't gotten Miranda ferrets. He'd gotten her gerbils. Which meant that Albert belonged to Georgie. Which meant that I had accidentally taken Georgie's pet.

Turn around, I told myself. *Turn around and tell Georgie what happened. Tell him you sort of accidentally found yourself in his room, and you sort of accidentally took his ferret.*

"Miranda said you would really like the gerbils," Josh said. "Cause you're really kind to animals."

I loosened my grip on Albert. I took lots of deep breaths. *You can do this*, I told myself. *You can tell him the truth.*

But then I thought of something else. What if he told Miranda?

I looked down at Albert's moist, sniffing nose. Miranda would not be happy. She didn't like mean people or lying people or people who crawled into other people's bedrooms. Even if they didn't do it on purpose.

"I have to go inside now," I said. Then I ran up my porch steps and into my house without looking back.

"Sylvie?" my mom called as soon as I shut the door.

"Just a minute!" I shouted, because if my mom saw Albert, she would scream and hit him with the flyswatter.

I ran down the hallway, away from my mom, away from the front door where Georgie might be lurking. My bedroom door was open. I looked inside, searching for a place to hide Albert. Somewhere safe where he couldn't drown or choke or get electrocuted. But it was no use. My room was full of dangerous things like outlets and seashells and tape. I couldn't leave him in here.

"Aha!" I said as an idea fell on top of me. What I needed was a ferret babysitter. Someone to watch Albert and keep him safe while I got a new birthday present for Miranda.

The twins. They were my only hope, so I hurried to their room and found them sitting on the floor, throwing packing peanuts into each other's mouths. I shut their door behind me and locked it. "Hi," I said. I held Albert up in the air. "I need you guys to watch this for me, okay?"

They began to cry in delight (in the case of Tate) and in fear (in the case of Cale).

"Shh!" I said firmly. "It's just a ferret. Not a goblin or anything."

They both went silent as they looked Albert over from head to tail. While they were examining him, I checked out their room. The boys have a fort in their closet they never clean up. It's made of old suit-cases and boxes and broken bicycle wheels and baby blankets, and it's practically indestroyable. Nothing gets in and nothing gets out.

"I'm going to put the ferret in your fort," I told the twins. "His name is Albert. And I'm borrowing him for a few minutes. Don't touch him. Don't hurt him. Don't tell Mom about him. We have to keep him perfectly safe." I looked at Cale, who was cowering on top of Tate's bed. "He won't hurt you," I promised.

"We'll take care of him," Tate said, but he looked a little too eager, like a hunter just spotting his prey.

"Don't touch him," I said again, with large, threatening eyes. "He doesn't belong to us. Okay?"

"Okay," Tate said, but I could see his fingers crossed behind his back.

"Sylvie!" my mom called again.

"No touching!" I said as I hurried out of the room. My mom had her I'm-going-to-make-Sylvie-do-jobs voice on, and the longer I took, the more jobs I would get.

"Boy, Mom, I'm really busy," I said when I found her in the kitchen, making something for lunch that looked suspiciously like mustard. "Too busy to help you with anything."

She looked up when I said this, the right side of her face scrunched up. When my mom scrunches up the right side of her face, it means she isn't happy with my attitude, so I tried to change it.

"I mean, I have lots of things to do after I help you with something." I smiled obediently. "Do you think later, after I do something for you, you could take me to the toy store?"

"Why?" my mom said, stirring her mustard ferociously.

"Because I need to get Miranda a different present for her birthday."

"What's wrong with the present you already got her?"

"It's a terrible present!" I cried. "Awful! Miranda will hate it. She'll open it up and she'll look at it, and she'll pretend to be nice and everything, but she'll hate it." I pounded my fist on the counter. "It's not nearly as good as gerbils!"

My mom sighed and put down her mustard spoon. Then she stepped to the kitchen table and pulled out two chairs, one for each of us. After arranging them neatly, she sat down and patted the seat next to her.

I love having chats with my mom, but not when she is patting the seat next to her. Patting the seat next to her means I've done something wrong and she wants to talk about it. I didn't want to sit down, but I had to.

"You seem to be struggling today," my mom began. "You didn't tell me where you were going this morning. You didn't come when I called you. And now you want to throw away a perfectly good present to get a different present for Miranda. One she probably won't like any better than the candles. The Sylvie I know wouldn't do these things."

I was trying to be nice so I wouldn't get into any more trouble, but it was hard. I wasn't the Sylvie she knew anymore. I was a stressed Sylvie. A dumb Sylvie. A Sylvie who accidentally took ferrets from mean boys' houses. A Sylvie who was about to lose her best friend. "I just want to get Miranda a great present," I said.

"Then what's going on between you and Miranda?"

I looked up at her then, because I wasn't expecting that question. She was tilting her head and looking at me with a sad face, and I knew that I could tell her right then. I could tell her everything, except for the part about accidentally taking Albert. I could tell her about Miranda and how she was becoming friends with Georgie, and if she became friends with Georgie, she wouldn't need me anymore.

But I knew what would happen next. Mom wouldn't understand. She'd talk about how Miranda would always be my friend and she would always need me, even if she did become friends with Georgie, and how I was worrying too much. And this made me mad.

"Nothing's going on," I said. "I just want to get her a nice present. That's all."

"Um-hmm," my mom said, like she didn't believe me.

"Really, Mom!"

"Sylvie, I know that Miranda is your first real best friend."

"No, she's not!" I said, even though she was.

"And I know things with friends can be confusing sometimes —"

"I'm not confused."

"— but Miranda is still going to want to be your friend, even if your present is not the most wonderful present in the world."

I frowned. I crossed my arms. I hated this conversation. I hated it.

With a sigh, she stood up and put her hand on my shoulder. "You'll see," she said.

I shook off her hand, even though I wanted it to stay there. "I have to go over to Georgie's house now. Is that okay?" I had to return Albert immediately. Before things got any worse.

The right side of Mom's face scrunched up at me again, even though I'd already fixed my attitude.

"All right," she said. "But don't be gone long."

Chapter 6

To the twins' dismay, I retrieved Albert from their
closet.

"No!" Tate shouted.

"Oh, man!" Cale said.

"It's okay," I told them. "One day you can get a ferret of your own. When you move out of the house and live somewhere without Mom."

Tate kicked his dresser. "That's going to take, like, three years!"

After giving them these words of comfort, I put Albert in a Florida Oranges box I found in the garage, slid the box lid on top, and began my march of death over to Georgie's house. It felt as if everyone in the world was watching me. Neighbors sitting at their windows. People doing yard work. Mosquitoes.

I made it across the street, and I made it up Georgie's front walk. But that's where I got stuck. I could hear noises inside. People sorts of noises.

My head was pounding, my heart was pounding. The front walk seemed to be pounding too.

"I'll check the porch," someone who sounded very much like Georgie shouted from inside.

"Shoot!" I said. I wasn't ready to tell Georgie about Albert. I needed time to think this out. To practice my speech. There was a big, fat bush right next to the porch steps. I shoved the box behind it and made it to the front door just as Georgie pulled it open.

"Oh!" he said. He blinked. He looked astonished. "Scruggs!"

Miranda appeared at Georgie's side. Behind them both was Josh.

"Oh, good!" Miranda said. She turned to Georgie. "I told you she would come."

"I didn't know you were here," I said. How could I return Albert if Miranda was there?

"I'm helping look for Georgie's ferret," she explained. She hurried down the porch steps, put her arm through mine, and made me walk into the house with her. "Dave was missing when Georgie got back from my house earlier. He brought me gerbils — oh, Sylvie, you'll love them! One is black and white, just like a cow, and I thought you could name —"

"I know about the gerbils," I said, so she would stop talking about them.

"My ferret's name isn't just Dave," Georgie said. "It's Dave Thomas, founder of Wendy's. Dave Thomas is the guy who made up the Wendy's place where they sell hamburgers. My dad met him once, so we decided to name Dave after him. Because Dave likes hamburgers."

Georgie kept on talking about Dave then. How great Dave was. How smart. How funny. My head was starting to hurt. My eyes were getting fuzzy. I wanted to tell him the truth. But my mouth wouldn't open.

"We've already searched the main level," Miranda said when Georgie was finally through.

"Why don't you search the basement next?" That was Georgie's grandma talking. She was standing in the room next to the front door, sorting laundry. The room had an enormous window that looked out onto the front yard, right over the bushes where Albert was hidden.

Georgie looked worried. "If Dave is in the basement, he might be in trouble. He might have found some rat poison. Or worse."

Miranda looked at me, her eyebrows scrunched together. She knows I don't go into basements, because goblins live in basements. Even though goblins aren't real. "Why don't you go search Georgie's room one more time, Sylvie? We don't need four people searching the basement."

So I walked down the hall with Georgie, where he practically shoved me into his room. He didn't give me a chance to say, "Wait! I know where Albert is! He's in an orange box in your bushes."

"Wait —" I said as Georgie ran down the hallway toward the basement.

But it was too late. Georgie was gone, and now Miranda thought I was helping look for Albert. "Why didn't you tell us right away?" she would say if I told the truth now. "Why did you take Albert home at all? What is the matter with you?"

"I don't know," I said to nobody.

I had to get Albert out of the bushes before Dagger sniffed him out and ate him, but I couldn't just walk out Georgie's front door. Georgie's grandma was standing right beside it. She'd watch me pick the orange box up out of the bushes, and then she'd wonder why I was storing oranges in her bushes. She might open the door and say, "Why are you storing oranges in my bushes?"

A stream of sunlight from Georgie's window suddenly shone on my face.

Georgie's window!

That was it — I could climb out Georgie's window, crawl over to the bushes so Georgie's grandma couldn't see me, and rescue Albert from Dagger. Even better, I could get Albert and slip him back into Georgie's room. Then Albert would be found, and Georgie would never know I'd taken him at all. And neither would Miranda.

Georgie's window was shut, of course, and locked. The lock was in the middle of the window. Even stretched up on my tippy-toes, I couldn't reach it, so I pushed Georgie's desk chair over to make me taller.

Still I couldn't reach it. So I got Georgie's pillow, an old shoe box, a book, and a pile of sweat-shirts, and stacked them on top of one another. I climbed on top, got on my

tiptoes, stretched my arm up as far as it would go, and at last, I could reach the lock.

I remembered how you unlock things, lefty-loosey, righty-tighty, pushed the lock to the left, and smiled at the sound of the window unlocking.

"Hello?" said a big scary man-voice.

I yelped and tumbled off the chair, landing on my hands and knees on top of a pile of LEGOs.

"Ow!" I said.

Georgie's dad left the doorway and came two steps closer. "Are you all right?" Georgie's dad was a muscley dad, twice the size of mine. He took another step toward me.

Every particle of my knees and hands hurt, thanks to the LEGOs, and I was pretty sure I was bleeding internationally, but I got to my feet anyway. "I'm fine," I said without looking at his face. "You don't have to do anything."

Georgie's dad coughed. "Okay. You must be one of Georgie's friends. Are you helping look for Dave?"

I stared at Georgie's messy floor. "I haven't seen Dave anywhere in this room," I said carefully.

Georgie's dad coughed again. "Well, I suppose I should leave you to your, um, search." Then he pretty much ran out of the room.

I didn't bother to watch where he was going. I didn't even bother to shut the door. Anyone could pop into the room at any moment, and I had to hurry. My hands shook as I put Georgie's things back on his bed. They trembled as I picked up the chair.

And that's when I saw it. The box. Sitting on top of Georgie's dresser next to too many old baseball trophies. A tall box wrapped in shiny silver wrapping paper, a white ribbon, and a bow.

A present. It hadn't been there before. There'd been nothing on Georgie's dresser before except dusty trophies and potato chip wrappers. *A birthday present,* I thought.

I knocked the chair over again in my hurry toward the box. There was a tag on top with a silver smiley face. I lifted the tag just enough to read it. *To Miranda,* it said. *Have the happiest of birthdays, Georgie.*

"Sylvie!" I heard Miranda call.

"I'm in here!" I said, rushing into the hall so Miranda wouldn't come into the room and see the box and know that Georgie had bought her another present.

"I have to go," I told her as I met her in the hall. "But tell Georgie that he will find Albert, I mean, Dave, really soon, so he doesn't have to be sad about it." I leaned in closer. "You can just go home right now, if you want. You really don't need to look for him."

Miranda gave me a sad look. "You have to go? Right now? I was hoping you could stay. Georgie still needs help looking — and you're the best looker I know."

"I can't stay," I said. "But I'll see you tomorrow. At your birthday party. And I'll have a really great present for you too. You'll love it!"

"Sounds perfect," she said. But she was already walking away, looking for Georgie.

Chapter 7

I nearly left Albert and the orange box in the bushes, because surely someone would find him at some point. But it might take a long time, and Dagger was outside in his yard with his pretend fence, snarling at me like a lion with a stomachache. He knew where Albert was, and if he got the chance, he would eat him.

Georgie's grandma was missing from the front window, so I snatched up the box as fast as I could and ran back home as if Albert's life depended on it.

After leaving Albert in the twins' fort, I went to my room to think. *Albert's fine,* I told myself as I flopped onto my bed. He'd only been missing from Georgie's for a few hours, and Georgie wasn't really that sad. Not yet. Georgie's window was unlocked now, so I could return Albert later that night, when everyone in the world, even Dagger, was asleep. Georgie would wake up to the best surprise of his life in the morning.

But then there was that box. The box with the silver wrapping paper. It was stuck in my brain like gum on a shoe. It was so large and square and expensive-looking. I thought about it while I helped my mom clean up the kitchen, I thought about it while I chewed my sausagey pizza, and I thought about it as I ate my Moose Tracks ice cream.

What could be in a box that big?

Later that night, after watching the twins play beef-jerky catch with Albert, I had a talk with my dad while we did the dishes. "I have to get a new present for Miranda," I told him.

Because he is my dad, and not my mom, he just said, "Really?"

"Yes," I said. "The best present ever."

"The best present ever," he said, rubbing his chin like he was thinking about it. "That's a tough order."

"I know," I said. Then I rinsed pepperoni grease off a plate and waited for him to tell me what to do. "Well?" I said when he didn't.

"Well, what?" he said.

"What should I do? I don't have any money. And Mom won't buy me another one."

"Then you'll have to make her something."

"Make her something?" I was stunned. Flabbergasted. "I can't make her something," I said. *Definitely nothing as good as gerbils or a giant silver box*, I thought.

"Now, now," he said, flapping a dish towel in my face. "The best presents are the homemade ones. Anyone can go to a store and plunk down some money and buy something —"

"Anyone who has money," I said.

"Yes, of course, but it is the rare friend indeed who will take the time to make her friend a homemade present. It's much more meaningful."

While my dad began telling me about the horse his dad carved for him out of a bar of soap — he'd named it Sudsy — I thought about this. Making something sounded nice. Like giving away your Christmas presents to kids who didn't get any.

But would Miranda really want me to make something for her?

"What would I make her?" I asked my dad.

He was in the middle of telling me about Sudsy's best friend, Bubbles, so it took him a moment to come up with an answer. "What would you buy her if you had money?" he said.

That was easy. "A gigantic castle to hold all her specimens. Her other one's too small now."

"Then that's what you should make her," he said.

In my room was an enormous tub of long, skinny blocks, the kind that balance so well you can build a tower as high as your ceiling.

I couldn't return Albert until it got dark, so right away I got busy. I found a square of plywood in the garage, got my mom's (off-limits) glue gun, and a giant (off-limits) bottle of glitter. I spread newspaper on the floor, because I am a responsible individual who doesn't want to get glitter on the carpet and face a lifetime in Mom Prison.

I began building my castle.

It would be huge. Better than one you could buy at a toy store. It would have fourteen towers, a drawbridge, and a sludgy, monster-filled moat. Even Albert would love it. If ferrets loved castles, which they probably did.

Building the foundation was easy. I made the outline of a giant square on the plywood and glued the blocks together. I was halfway done with the walls when I realized I'd forgotten to leave a space for the drawbridge, so I had to tear apart one wall. Which made the one next to it crumble. I had almost fixed that problem when I realized that none of the walls had windows. But the walls were already built, so I would need a saw to make them.

This was a problem. I was afraid of saws because they reminded me of goblin teeth, even though

71

goblins aren't real. So I got a knife from the kitchen and tried that. But knives are good at cutting the skin on your fingers, not making windows.

It wasn't until the north-south wall fell over into a heap of useless blocks and stringy glue that I lost my temper and smashed down the entire castle. Or what was left of it.

The doorbell rang.

The air vent in my room is right over the entry-way. I listened carefully as my dad answered the door. "Oh, hello! Josh, isn't it? How nice to see you. What's that you've got?"

"A casserole," Josh said. "My mom had extra. It's got mushrooms and steak. She put it in this disposable pan, so you can freeze it if you want. For when the baby comes."

Josh's mom was famous in the neighborhood for sharing casseroles. This could be a good thing or a bad thing, depending on the casserole. Mushrooms made this a bad thing.

"Would you like to come in?" my dad said.

I fell forward in surprise, my hands pressing painfully against some blocks.

"I believe Sylvie's in her room," my dad said, and before I could shout "No, no, no! Josh cannot come in my room!" my door was opening.

"Oh, dear," my dad said when he stepped inside

and saw the mess on the floor and the glue on my hands. "Are you all right, honey?"

Normally I would have screamed that I was not all right, and this castle was never going to work because I was terrible at building things, and I might as well go rob the toy store. Jail would be better than trying to build a castle for Miranda. But Josh was in my room, so I just nodded and sniffed and waited for them to go away and shut the door so I could scream in my own privacy.

"What are you making?" Josh said, like nothing was wrong. And then he said two shocking words. "A castle?"

My mouth dropped like a bouncy ball. I looked at my dad, but he just shrugged and left the room. The traitor.

"I made a castle once, out of blocks," Josh said. "My sister helped me. We made a drawbridge too. Do you have any cardboard?"

I did have cardboard. Our garage is practically a cardboard box warehouse, and before I knew it, Josh was selecting the perfect cardboard for the drawbridge, and I was building a castle with Josh Stetson. In my room. With a glue gun and even glitter. We built the foundation and walls and towers out of blocks. The moat was made of sludgy blue paper. We decorated the dungeon with bits of coal, also found in the garage. Josh went bonkers with the glitter, sprinkling it everywhere until the entire castle sparkled. He even knew how to make windows without a saw.

"Thanks," I heard myself saying when we were through.

"Miranda will love it," Josh said, and my mouth dropped again, like another bouncy ball.

"How did you know I was making this for Miranda?" I said. Then I gasped. "Are you spying for Georgie?"

"Huh?" Josh said. "No — I just guessed it was for Miranda because her birthday's tomorrow, and she

has that castle in her room that's too small." He got to his feet. "I'll see you tomorrow."

"Hmm," I said suspiciously instead of saying good-bye, but he left anyway.

I watched him walk slowly down the path, his head pointing down, his shoulders pointing up, like he didn't want to leave. What if Josh was working for Georgie? What if Georgie had sent him over here — with the casserole for cover — so he could find out what I was getting for Miranda? Georgie would want to know. He'd want to know so he could make sure his present was better.

But at least he didn't see Albert. If Josh saw Albert, he would tell Georgie, and Georgie would tell Miranda, and Miranda would ask why, and I wouldn't be able to answer her, and she would say "We're not going to be friends anymore, Sylvie Scruggs. Not forever and ever. Not for all the castles in the universe."

Chapter 8

"Let's put the castle in the wagon," my dad said when he was through admiring my work. Okay, mine and Josh's work. We lugged the castle out to the garage together. "That way you can just pull it over to Miranda's in the morning," he explained.

The castle was so enormous, it barely fit inside the wagon's metal bottom, and our wagon was a

big wagon, big enough for three or four kids to ride in at once. "This is a really good present," my dad said. "Miranda's crazy if she doesn't love it."

"Miranda's not crazy," I said.

Tate and Cale poked their heads into the garage to see what we were doing.

"Wowzers," Cale said. "That's cool!"

"Can we have it?" Tate said. "Albert would love it. Especially the moat. He loves to swim."

"Who's Albert?" my dad said, trying to ruffle Tate's hair without getting bitten. "One of your stuffed animals?"

"Stuffed animals?" Cale said.

"Huh?" Tate said.

"Yes," I said as I pinched Tate's elbow and stepped on Cale's toe. "They have a stuffed ferret named Albert who loves castles." I looked at them hard. "Remember? Your stuffed ferret? Because he's not real, he's stuffed."

Tate and Cale looked at me like their brains had been erased, so I told my dad I would put them to bed, and after a stern lecture about not giving away important secrets, I did. Then I found a soft blue blanket (blueish/greenish is Miranda's favorite color) to cover up the castle. It fit perfectly. Silver is Miranda's other favorite color, so I found four silver bows in the gift-wrap box and set them on top of every tower. Silver bows are better than silver wrapping paper, because you can save them afterward.

Happy shivers ran through my body as I stepped back to look at my creation. But I didn't have time for happy shivers. I had to return Albert. Tonight.

When my dad tucked me in later, I pretended to be very, very sleepy. But I wasn't sleepy. I was listening to my parents put the house to bed.

"Did you get the front door?" my mom said like she always does.

"Yes, did you lock the back?" my dad said like he always does.

"Yes, get the lights, please," my mom said like she always does.

My dad's voice got low. "Roger that, Captain."

Then, like it always does, my door opened.

"She's out," my dad said. "Funny girl — how was she today? On a scale of one to ten?"

My mom sighed like she always does. "No major disasters to report. Just worrying about things she doesn't need to worry about. Like usual."

After this rude comment, my door shut and my parents made their loud and regular noises of checking on the twins and brushing their teeth and going to the bathroom.

When the gigantic metal floor fan in their bedroom turned on, I knew I was safe. That fan is loud enough to block out the sounds of one hundred snarling lions, so I flipped over in bed and watched my clock as it moved from ten fifteen to ten sixteen to ten seventeen. . . .

At eleven o'clock p.m. time, I popped right up and climbed out of bed. My hands shook as I put on my blackest clothes. My heart thumped as I pulled my hair into a ponytail. I was so nervous I almost gave myself the hiccups as I snuck into the boys'

room. This was my last chance to put Albert back before Miranda's party.

"Sylvie?"

Shoot. It was Cale.

"Go back to sleep," I said.

"Why are you in our room?" Cale said.

"Why are you wearing those clothes?" Tate said.

"Shhh!" I said in a furious whisper. "You'll wake up Mom and Dad."

"They can't hear anything with Mom's lion fan on," Tate said.

"All right, all right," I said. "I'm returning Albert, that's all."

"Right now?" Cale said. "In the night?"

"I want to come." Tate sat up really fast and banged his head on Cale's bunk. "Ow!"

"I don't think we should go anywhere in the dark," Cale said. "There could be bad guys out there."

"I'm coming," Tate said cheerfully.

"You're not coming," I said, because that would be a disaster. They would make too much noise. Then Georgie's dad would call the cops. Dagger would wake up. "I was just kidding about returning him. I'm going to keep Albert in my room tonight." I paused to think of a good reason. "Because I'm lonely."

"Lonely?" Tate and Cale both began talking at once because they don't know what it means to be lonely. They always have each other.

I scooped up the sleeping ferret and ignored him when he bit my finger.

"Good night!" I said. "I'll see you tomorrow. Have some nice dreams!"

Then I shut the door behind me. I waited for several seconds, to make sure they went back to sleep. When no sounds came from their room, not even whispering, I tiptoed to the garage to get a nice box for Albert, one a little more comfortable than the orange box, which didn't smell too good anymore. I found some newspaper and some old rags, and pretty soon had him very comfortable for our trip across the street.

This is easy, I thought as I snuck out the side garage door. The moon was out, so the dark wasn't too scary. I'd just walk on over and drop Albert off, no problem.

I didn't see Tate and Cale until they were standing next to me on the sidewalk in their pajamas with black stuff on their faces.

"Permanent marker," Tate said with an evil grin. He pointed to the black streaks on his forehead and cheeks. "For camouflage."

"I didn't have time to do a very good job because Tate got the marker first," Cale said. His face didn't

have black streaks, just black dots. He looked like a chocolate-chip ice cream cone.

"All right, all right," I said. "I guess you can come. But the rule is you must not speak. Not at all. Not a peep. Not even if you trip and break your leg. Not even if you see a dangerous monster about to eat you. Not even if the police capture you and take you to the police station and make you eat mushrooms until you tell them the truth." I paused dramatically. "Got it?" I waited for them to run away in terror.

"Got it," Tate said.

"Got it," Cale said.

"Okay," I said, giving up. "But you have to be perfectly quiet." I stepped off the sidewalk. Cale stepped off the sidewalk. Tate stepped off the sidewalk.

"Ow, Tate! You stepped on my foot," Cale said.

"I did not," Tate said, not even bothering to whisper. "You just stepped on your own foot. And a slug."

"Ew!" Cale shouted, because he hated slugs. "Ew, ew, ew! Get it off, Sylvie. Get the slug off my shoe."

This conversation continued all the way to Georgie's house, and despite the number of times I pinched their elbows, it continued until we were standing in the backyard.

"You have to be quiet now," I told them. "If we get caught, they could toss me into prison and throw away the key. Do you understand?"

"Where would they throw the key?" Tate said.

"Why don't you just give Albert back?" Cale said. "In the daytime. At the front door."

"Because I can't," I said, louder than I should have. "It was an accident — this wasn't my fault. Now stop talking."

Cale zipped his lips. "I won't talk again," he grunted through his teeth.

Tate reluctantly did the same. "All right," he said through sealed lips. "I won't talk either."

"Okay," I said, keeping my teeth shut. "See that bucket?"

"What?" Cale said through shut teeth.

"She said, 'Do you see that bucket?'" Tate said, also through shut teeth.

"What?" Cale said.

"Okay," I said. "We can whisper, but the whisper must be so soft only a lizard could hear it." Lizards have super sensitive ear drummers, according to Miranda.

I hunched over. Cale hunched over. Tate hunched over. Our faces were nearly touching. "Cale is Mr. Stink Breath," Tate said in a whisper.

"Am not!" Cale whispered back.

"Quiet," I ordered, though Cale's breath really was stinky. Then I explained the situation: stand on bucket, open bedroom window, slip Albert inside. Tate was assigned to hold Albert's box while Cale was to help me move the bucket. But it was dark, and I couldn't remember for sure which window was Georgie's.

"Is that it?" Cale asked as I tried the first window.

"Window locks should be on the outside," I said, because the stupid window wouldn't open. "It must be the next one."

"Is that it?" Cale asked as I pulled and tugged on the next window.

"No," I said. "It's not. And stop asking me questions. I can't concentrate. It's not easy to open windows."

"Are you sure you unlocked the window?" Tate said. "Maybe you locked it."

"I'm sure," I whispered surely. "I don't get stuff like that wrong, Tate. Lefty-loosey. Righty-tighty."

Tate looked stunned at these words of wisdom. Cale looked hungry.

I ignored them both. I knew I had unlocked Georgie's window, and there was only one possibility left. I crossed my fingers as Cale and I moved the bucket. I stepped up. I put my fingers on the side of the window thingy. I pulled with every last bit of strength I'd ever had since I was born.

"No," I said, when it wouldn't budge. "No, no, no!"

"Sylvie!" Cale whispered. "Stop shouting!"

"That grandma's a crazy window-locking person!" I said, still pulling on the window. "She must go around the house locking windows just for fun. It's not as if there's crime in this neighborhood! It's not as if someone is going to climb in the window and steal stuff!"

Dagger woke up with a roar so loud, the ground practically shook.

"Ahhhhhh!" Cale shouted, and he dove out of the bushes and ran toward our house as fast as his short legs could carry him.

I looked at Tate with serious eyes that said "Don't you dare run off screaming too." But he dropped Albert's box on the ground and took off after Cale. "Ruff, ruff," he shouted at Dagger.

I picked Albert up and started to follow, but a screeching sound came from the house. I paused.

The sound kept coming. Georgie's back door was opening.

I screamed without making any noise and took off around the house like a girl afraid to get caught by a muscley dad or a window-locking grandma or a friend-stealing boy.

Chapter 9

Morning arrived — the birthday party morning. Albert had now been at my house for a really long time. Overnight even. There was no way I could just walk up to Georgie and tell him the truth. He'd been searching for Albert all day yesterday. He probably hadn't slept last night. And there was no Albert waiting for him in the morning like I'd planned.

"Maybe I should be sick," I said to myself as I lay in my bed.

I couldn't face Georgie knowing Albert was still at my house. "Maybe I am sick."

I was seeing if I could throw up when my mom came into the room. "I thought you'd be up by now on a big day like this." She rubbed her stomach. "Miranda's mother just called to ask if you'd like to come over early to help get ready for the party."

"Really?" I sat up in bed. "How early? Like now early?"

"Yes, honey. Like now early."

"What else did she say? Will anyone else be there?"

My mom groaned a little and shifted her feet. "I have no idea, but it sounded like they really want some help."

I swung my legs over the side of the bed. This was perfect. I could go over early — before Georgie got there, so I wouldn't have to see him — give Miranda her present, then get sick. Then Miranda would be thinking about my enormous castle the whole party. She'd never forget about me!

"Get dressed first and get a bite to eat," my mom

said, giving me a kiss and another groan before leaving the room.

I was just putting on my shoes when another great idea popped into my head. I could give Albert back while Georgie was at the party. I could leave him on the porch in his box. He'd be too far away for Dagger to smell on the porch, and Georgie would be coming home soon, so Albert wouldn't be there long. It would work perfectly unless Georgie's grandma was standing at that window again, folding more laundry.

Miranda was hanging a giant stick bug on the front door when I pulled the wagon up to her porch. As soon as she saw me she put down her supplies and gave me a tight birthday hug. "What's that?" she said, pointing at the castle still wrapped up in its blanket.

My cheeks went warm. I couldn't look at her face. It's easy to know your present is amazing when you're alone in your garage wrapping it in a blanket. It's harder to know your present is amazing when your best friend is wondering what it is. "It's your present," I said. "I made it."

Miranda isn't impressed by much because she's a scientist, but, at that moment, every muscle in her face looked impressed. "Wow," she said. "That's huge. But I don't think we can get it inside my house." She clasped her hands together as an idea jumped into her brain. "I know! We can put it in the garage like it's a secret discovery no one knows about. Then we can pull it out at the very end of the party, and everyone will be so surprised. I'll go open the garage."

While Miranda ran inside the house, I thought about what to say to her. *Could you open my present now? Because I'm starting to feel sick.* But that wouldn't work. Miranda had three thermometers and a magnifying glass in her castle/laboratory, and she'd want to take my temperature and see my throat.

I pulled the wagon over to the garage. I'd have to leave before Miranda opened my present. I wouldn't be able to see her face when she took off the blanket. But I didn't want to see Georgie until Albert was back home.

"Hey, Scruggs," came a voice from behind me.

No way. I closed my eyes. *Disappear,* I thought. *Go back home. Forever and ever and ever.*

"What's with the wagon?" Georgie said.

"I like wagons." That was Josh's voice.

Georgie took a step closer so I could see him out of the corner of my eye. He was holding the horrible silver box. "We still haven't found Dave Thomas, founder of Wendy's. I'm really worried — he must be starving. He probably hasn't eaten for days."

I turned away so Georgie couldn't see my face. I'd given Albert water and food. Lots of food — even ice cream. Albert was fine. Perfectly fine.

The garage door began to rise.

"Miranda invited us over to help fill water balloons," Josh said.

Georgie nodded. "So I wouldn't worry about Dave so much." I turned to look at him then. He didn't sound very worried. He didn't look very worried. His cheeks weren't wet and his eyes weren't red like they should be. "What's under the blanket?" he said.

"Don't touch it," Josh and I said.

Miranda ran through the garage and onto the driveway. "That's my present from Sylvie," she told

Georgie. "She's going to hide it in the garage. Wow, that's big."

Miranda was not pointing to my castle as she said this. She was pointing to the silver box. Her face muscles looked impressed all over again.

Georgie shrugged. "And heavy. Can I put it inside?"

Miranda nodded happily and motioned us toward the garage door. Georgie went first, like this was his house and his birthday party.

I looked over at my house, where Albert was waiting patiently to go home. The twins were watching him for me in the fort. If I left him on Georgie's porch right now, there was a chance Dagger might get him. Or a raccoon or a cat. I could stay at Miranda's for a little while longer. Georgie wouldn't know Albert was back until he got home anyway.

"You go ahead," Josh said, making me jump.

For just a few minutes, I thought, before running after Georgie.

Chapter 10

Birthday parties were a big deal at Miranda's. Her mom decorated the front porch and the hallways and the backyard. The table was set with special napkins, plates, and cups, and there was always a fancy cake ordered from the bakery. (Birthday parties at my house were not a big deal. My mom made a cake from a box, had us play tag outside, and let us watch a movie after we opened presents. When I complained about the unfairness of this, my mom said I could move to an only-child family any day I wanted to.)

My whole body tingled as I walked inside and looked around. The Tans' house had been transformed into Insect World for the party. Miranda's giant bugs hung on the walls and from the ceiling.

The house plants had been moved into the family room, and green and brown crepe paper and balloons were everywhere you looked. It was a bug jungle.

Miranda assigned Georgie and Josh to fill up water balloons in the backyard with the hose. Then she asked me to stay inside with her to get the games ready, which made me tingle all over again.

Soon the five other girls Miranda had invited to the party arrived, giggling, congratulating Miranda on turning nine, and talking about the other birthday parties they had gone to that year. Even though I hadn't gone to any of them.

I should go now, I thought. I could say I forgot something, run home, drop off Albert, and come back to the party. But before everyone had even set down their presents, Miranda announced that it was time for games. "I'll need your help, Sylvie," she said.

"I can help," Georgie said.

"No, I can," I said. "I can help."

"You can both help," Miranda said. And we both sort of did, except I helped way better than Georgie, who seemed to have forgotten about Albert.

The games did not go well. Here is what happened:

Fishing Game
(where Mrs. Tan stands behind a blue sheet and we fish for presents)

I pulled up a rubber fly on my first try, a rubber mosquito on my second try, and a coconut-flavored lollipop on my third try. It was a huge coconut-flavored lollipop, but whoever makes coconut-flavored lollipops must actually think that coconut-flavored lollipops taste good. They do not. Georgie pulled up a chocolate gold coin on his first try, a chocolate gold coin on his second try, and a bag of chocolate gold coins on his third try. Mrs. Tan must have thought he was a pirate, which makes sense because he ate up all the coins in front of everyone without sharing.

Score: Sylvie — a big fat zero; Georgie — a big fat chocolate head.

Insect Charades
(a game where you act out particular kinds of insects)

I got stuck with Savannah, Rita, and Haley — whispery girls who never tell you what they're saying. Georgie got Josh, Miranda, Anna, and Jasmine — the kind of people who probably practice charades for fun. I had to act out a cicada and no one on my team knew what a cicada was. Not even me. Georgie had to act out a praying mantis. All he did was pretend to pray.

Score: Sylvie's Team — one (because Haley knew how to be a killer bee); Georgie's Team — five (because Miranda was on his team and she's practically an insectologist).

"I have to run home for a second," I told Miranda when charades were over.

But she wasn't listening. "Time for Water Balloon Dodgeball!"

"Water Balloon Dodgeball?" I said. We'd never played that before. "What's that?"

"It's Georgie's idea," Miranda said.

"It's awesome, Scruggs," Georgie said. "But you might not want to play. Water balloons are even harder to throw than baseballs."

Everything inside me went tight at those words. I was like a leopard ready to spring. "I can throw anything better than you," I said.

"Not a baseball," Georgie said.

Everyone went quiet. Even the whispery girls.

"I can definitely throw a water balloon better than you," I said.

"Are they mad at each other?" Anna whispered to Jasmine.

"I think so," Jasmine said.

"Sylvie?" Miranda said, like she wasn't too sure about this.

But at that moment, I didn't care. I didn't care what those whispery girls said, and I didn't even care what Miranda said. I was mad. Georgie was trying to make me look stupid. He was trying to steal my best friend, my only best friend, right out from under my chin. "You don't deserve Albert," I muttered.

"Huh?" Georgie said.

Minutes later, the two teams were lined up, facing each other over no-man's-land, a strip of lawn no one could cross during the game. Josh was on my team. Miranda was on Georgie's. Everyone had a balloon in their hands.

When Georgie blew the whistle he'd brought just for this, I picked up a water balloon and hurled it right at his face. It missed his face, but hit him smack in the stomach.

Ha, I thought. Then I said it out loud. "Ha!"

While I was saying "Ha!" again, Georgie threw his water balloon at me. I ducked, and it hit Josh in the arm, breaking apart and soaking his shirt.

I looked at Georgie and ha'd one more time. His smirk turned into a look of rage.

He picked up another water balloon and so did I.

I chucked mine hard and got him again, first try.
He pitched one at me, and it nearly got me, but I did
a side-somersault roll, the kind you see on TV, and
it missed.

Ha.

The fighting continued like that: Georgie trying
to get me, me trying to get Georgie, Josh trying to
get Georgie too, Miranda and the whispery girls
throwing balloons at anything that moved. Not a
single balloon touched me the entire game. Not

Georgie's. Not Miranda's. Not anyone's. And it wasn't just because Josh kept getting in my way, though Georgie said it was.

When Mrs. Tan poked her head out of the kitchen to call us for lunch, the score was obvious. Georgie's shirt was soaked and most of his shorts. Even his hair was drippy.

I was completely dry, and if you are dry at the end of Water Balloon Dodgeball, you win.

There were still two water balloons left in Georgie's bucket and one in mine. I picked mine up. "Think you can dodge this?" I said to Georgie.

Georgie picked up both of his, and with a roar, he crossed no-man's-land and ran right at me.

I am a better pitcher than Georgie, but he is a better runner, so even though I turned and ran as fast as I could, Georgie was right behind me, his footsteps pounding in my ears.

Dodgeball had worn me out more than I thought. My legs were weak. It hurt to breathe. But I couldn't give up. If I stopped, or worse, fell, Georgie wouldn't hesitate. He would throw both of his bal-loons right at me, and I'd be too exhausted to do anything about it.

We were almost to the back fence when I tripped. I fell right on my face, twisting my ankle and scraping my leg. There wasn't time to run away, so I cov-ered my head and my face and waited for Georgie to clobber me with his water balloons.

But he did not. "Geez, Scruggs. Are you all right?"

I lowered my arms enough to peek up at him. Both of the water balloons were in his left hand. His right hand was out, not like he wanted to arm-wrestle me, but like he wanted to help me up.

"Did you hurt your foot?" he said when I didn't move.

I didn't know what to do. It might be a trick, so I got to my feet as fast as I could. "I'm okay," I said. This was not exactly true. My ankle hurt a lot. A lot, a lot. But I didn't want Georgie to know this.

"Miranda," Mrs. Tan shouted from the kitchen window. "Will you please gather your friends at the picnic table?"

Georgie dropped his water balloons. They splatted on the ground — splash, splash.

"Are you all right, Sylvie?" Miranda called.

"Yes," I said, pretending not to limp as I headed toward her and away from Georgie. I didn't want him to laugh as he watched me go. "I'm fine," I said. "Perfectly fine."

Chapter 11

But I wasn't fine. The birthday party would be over soon, and I was running out of time to return Albert. Plus my ankle really hurt. I wouldn't be able to run across the street with Albert in his box. I wouldn't be able to drop it on the porch and get out of there as fast as I could. I'd have to hobble away as fast as I could, which might not be fast enough.

I was debating what to do when I saw my brothers' faces in Miranda's dining room window. They looked at me, then at each other. Then their faces disappeared.

"I'll be right back," I said to Miranda, who was already sitting down at the picnic table. By Georgie.

"What are you doing here?" I demanded when I found my brothers in the kitchen.

"Don't worry," Tate said. "Mom's at the doctor's and Albert is safe."

"He's way safe," Cale said. "Safer than ever. It's for a surprise."

"But don't worry," Tate said. "He's having fun. Way more fun than in the closet."

"Mom's at the doctor's?" I said. "Did she have a doctor's appointment?"

Mrs. Tan came into the room. She stopped fast at the sight of me. "Oh, Sylvie," she said. "I haven't had a second to tell you — and here are the twins." She was smiling, and I couldn't tell if it was a pretend-things-are-all-right kind of smile or a real one. "Your mother was having some funny pains, so your father's taken her to the doctor to check on the baby. I told him to send the twins over here."

"Pains?" I said. Okay, shrieked.

Mrs. Tan put an arm around my shoulders. "Don't look like that, sweetheart. Everything's going to be fine."

"No, it's not!" I said. "Pains are bad. You aren't supposed to have pains when you're pregnant. Something must be wrong!"

Mrs. Tan gave me a squeeze. "Your dad thinks it's just indigestion, but your mother wanted to be sure. Really, Sylvie, there's nothing to worry about."

"What's indigestion?" I demanded.

Mrs. Tan explained about indigestion and heartburn and what it feels like to be pregnant with a baby smashing your stomach. This was gross, but important. My mom had eaten four pieces of meat-lover's pizza for dinner last night, and she probably had a piece for breakfast. Indigestion made sense.

Mrs. Tan gave me a squeeze. "Now, I don't want you to worry about a thing. I'll update you when your father calls, and, boys, I've got some serious movies planned for you, but first, we're going to play with the gerbils and eat cake and ice cream and lunch in the playroom, away from the big kids. Sound good?"

Cale nodded because he loved cake and ice cream and staying away from big kids. Tate shook his head. "I don't like serious movies," he said. "But I'll play with the gerbils."

"I will escort them down to the playroom," I said.

"All right," Mrs. Tan said. "But, boys, remember. Your mother said no more permanent markers. No paint. You're not allowed to draw anything on your hands or faces. Or arms or legs. Or any part of your skin." She squinted at their bright pink cheeks and the faint black marks left over from last night.

"They will be skin-free," I said. Then I walked them down the hall as fast as my ankle would let me. "What happened?" I demanded. "Tell me everything."

Cale looked at Tate. Tate looked at me. "Mom was making lots of loud noises. Kind of like a horse."

Cale nodded. "And Dad was running around, looking for Tums."

"They were too busy to notice Albert," Tate said. "So we put him in Mom's bag."

"So we could do our surprise," Cale said. "Albert really likes bags. He made his funny gurgling noises as soon as we put him in there."

"You put him in Mom's bag?" Mom kept her hospital bag in the entryway. Just in case.

"Yeah, but Mom and Dad didn't see us do it. We were supersneaky."

"But where did you put the bag?" I cried. "Did you leave it in the entryway?"

"No," Tate said, like he would never do something that stupid.

"We left the bag in the garage," Cale said.

"In the garage?" I pictured them sticking the bag inside the garage. Dad would see it and toss it in the car. Then Mom would bring it inside the doctor's office. Albert would escape from the bag and begin running around a building full of sick people. He'd be chased by nurses with beeping machines, or doctors with big fat needles.

"Did we use the gray bag or black bag?" Cale asked Tate. "I can't remember."

Tate scrunched up his nose like he was thinking. "What gray bag?"

"You know," Cale said. "The one that's all gray. Not black."

Hands on my hips, I bent over so I could look them both right in the face. "Where is Albert?"

"Sylvie!" Mrs. Tan said, coming into the play-room. "They're waiting for you outside. And boys, I've got the gerbils and the movies and the yummy food ready. What do you say?"

"Sylvie's pinching my elbow," Tate said. "And it hurts."

"Oh!" I said, nicely brushing off his arm. "Sorry. I didn't see your elbow there. I guess I'll go outside now." I looked at Tate. He looked at me. "You can tell me more about Albert later," I said.

"No, I can't," he said, eyebrows wiggling. "It's a surprise."

Lunch took forever. I ate it because if I didn't, Miranda would be suspicious, but nothing tasted good. Except the Tater Tots. Albert was missing: maybe in a gray bag, maybe in a black bag. Maybe in the garage, maybe with my parents, maybe dead at the doctor's.

I needed to get home and get into the garage

somehow. Maybe I could smash a brick through the garage window and save Albert before my parents found him.

When we'd finally finished the cake and ice cream, I said, "I need to go check on something at home."

"What do you need to check?" Miranda said.

"Time to open presents!" Mrs. Tan called from the kitchen door. "I was going to have you come inside, but everyone's still too wet, so the presents are out on the driveway. Are you ready?"

"Yes!" Miranda cried. Then she looked at me. "Can you wait to go home until after we open presents? I'm so excited to see what's in the wagon."

I started to shake my head. I couldn't wait. It was now or never.

"Please?" Miranda said.

Chapter 12

On the driveway stood a stack of presents and a chair for Miranda. Mrs. Tan had laid a blanket out beside the chair for the rest of us to sit and watch the great present opening.

"We'll get the wagon out last," Miranda said as I sat down on a corner of the blanket. "Is that all right?"

No, I thought. *Do it first, so I can go home.* "Sure," I said with a worn-out sigh. Even if my parents had left our garage unlocked, and I found Albert there in the bag, I couldn't take him over to Georgie's. Not with everyone sitting on Miranda's driveway. They'd see me walking down the street. They'd see me walking across the street. They would see me and know I was up to no good.

Miranda began opening her gifts one by one. There was a real live karaoke machine, pom-poms, a fashion-design kit, and nail polish.

"Has my dad called?" I asked Mrs. Tan when this lame-o present had been opened.

Mrs. Tan shook her head at me. "Not yet."

Then Josh handed Miranda his gift. Miranda tore off the wrapping paper. It was a stuffed sea anemone. Josh pointed to the tag. "It's from the endangered species catalogue," he said. "When you buy one, you help save a real sea anemone."

"I love it!" Miranda said, and I could tell she did.

"Do you think my dad will call before they come home?" I asked Mrs. Tan.

"Probably," Mrs. Tan said unhelpfully.

Georgie's present was the last one in the pile. Miranda picked it up and said, "Wow, this is heavy."

"Heavy doesn't mean much," I said. "A rock could be heavy."

"Ooh, I like rocks," Miranda said as she ripped off the paper. She gasped. I leaned forward, looked at the box, and gasped in exactly the same way.

Georgie smiled, looking smug. "It's a microscope," he explained to everyone. " 'Cause Miranda likes science." Then he looked at me. "Remember?"

"No," I said, because I had no idea what he was talking about.

Until, suddenly, I did.

This was my fault. I had told him that Miranda loved science. Me. Sylvie Scruggs. I'd opened my big fat mouth when Georgie was giving her the goldfish and I told him something he wouldn't have figured out on his own.

Miranda looked like she might faint. "I've always wanted a microscope!" She began tearing into the box. "Oh my gosh!" she said. "It's huge! And it's not just one of those toy things you can buy online." She began to pull the microscope out.

A microscope. I had known Miranda wanted a microscope. She'd wanted one for years. But she

always told me that real microscopes were too expensive. "Are you sure it's real?" I said.

Even as I said it, I knew it was real. It was big and black, with lots of knobs and dials and things poking out everywhere.

"It was my *abuelo*'s," Georgie said with a shrug. "My *abuela* said we don't use it anymore, so Miranda could have it."

"That's very generous of your grandmother," Mrs. Tan said, and Georgie looked smug all over again, as if it was really generous of him.

I glanced up at Miranda's garage, where my castle lay waiting. What was I thinking? A homemade present! Nail polish was better. Candles were better. Blobs of wax would have been better.

"I guess it's time to go home," I said, pretending to be cheerful. "Sure was a great party!"

"But what about your present?" Josh said, and before I could stop him, he was running up to the garage and pulling my wagon down the driveway.

Mrs. Tan held out her arms to take the microscope from Miranda, but Miranda didn't let go. The phone began to ring inside the house. "I'd better get that," Mrs. Tan said, and she hurried away.

"Maybe we should all go," I said loudly. I could just imagine what Georgie would say when he saw my present. "A castle made of blocks?" Everyone would laugh at such a babyish gift.

"Here," Josh said, giving the handle of the wagon to Miranda. He pulled something black off his shoulder and tried to hand it to me. "This was in the wagon too."

I did not take the thing in his hand. I just stared at it, not moving. It was my mom's hospital bag. I looked at the wagon. The blanket was crooked, and the silver bows I'd placed so carefully on top were gone.

A gurgling noise came from somewhere below. I looked around my feet. I looked at the driveway. I looked at Georgie's stomach. The gurgling noise came again, louder this time.

I looked at the wagon.

"Albert would love to play in a castle," Tate had said.

"We left the bag in the garage," Cale had said.

"It's a surprise," Tate had said.

"Oh no," I whispered. They hadn't left the bag in our garage — they'd left it in Miranda's garage!

The microscope was on the ground. Miranda was standing up. She stretched her free hand toward the castle. "What was that noise?" she said as she yanked off the blanket.

"Wait!" I shouted. "Stop!"

But it was too late. There sat my sparkly, beautiful castle.

And there was Albert, sitting right in the middle of it.

"Dave!" Georgie shouted as Albert leaped out of the castle and scampered across the driveway. Georgie took off after him. Josh ran after Georgie. All three hurried across the lawn, heading for the backyard.

I wanted to chase after them, to help capture Albert, but I couldn't take my eyes off Miranda. Her body was bent toward the castle, probably examining it for a secret ferret entrance.

"How did Dave get in here?" she said to the castle.

"Yeah," Savannah said, looking right at me. "I thought Dave was missing."

"Since yesterday," Rita said. "Georgie told me."

Miranda looked perplexedous. "I don't think he was in my garage — and I don't think he could have climbed the castle walls on his own." She turned to me. "Did you put him in there?"

I shook my head.

Anna was standing right next to Miranda. "I bet she stole him," Anna whispered. "So she could put him in your castle."

"I could totally see Sylvie doing that," Jasmine said, not even bothering to whisper. "That's why I never invite her over to my house."

Miranda frowned and looked at the castle again. "No," she said. "Sylvie doesn't steal things. And she helped Georgie look for Dave yesterday."

Everyone turned toward me then, expecting an explanation. I opened my mouth. Then shut it. My face was hot. My mouth was dry. My tongue felt too fat to speak. I shook my head. Then I nodded.

"She's about to cry," someone whispered.

"Sylvie?" Miranda said.

I turned to her and only her. "It was an accident," I said. "I didn't mean to take him. I tried to put him back."

"You took him?" Miranda said. "How?"

"She means she stole him," Anna whispered in Miranda's ear.

"He was safe the whole time," I said, my voice getting louder. "He was in the twins' closet, and it wasn't that long. Just overnight. I took really good care of him."

"You can go to jail for stealing things," Anna said. "Georgie could call the police."

Miranda was in the middle of those girls now, right in the center of their circle. "I don't understand, Sylvie. Did you find him outside?"

"No," I said.

"Did you sneak into his house?" Jasmine said.

"Did you break in in the middle of the night?" Rita said.

"Look," Jasmine whispered. "She's really crying now."

"Sylvie?" Miranda said, looking so sad and worried. Like I had broken her heart. "Did you steal Dave?"

"Yes," I said. "I did. I stole him, okay? He was in Georgie's room, and I climbed inside and I took him! Because I'm a bad person. A horrible, bad person who can't be your best friend!"

"Sylvie!" Mrs. Tan said. She was standing next to me, her arms crossed tight.

My parents' car turned onto our street at that exact moment. It was heading our way, so I took off across the Tans' lawn, across the street, running as fast and as hard as I could, my ankle hurting the whole way.

Chapter 13

I tried to escape up to my room without talking to anyone, but my mom took one look at my face as I raced past her in the garage and said, "Sylvie!"

And my dad said, "Is she crying, Claire? I think she's crying."

Then they followed me into the house and into the hall.

"Honey, I'm fine," my mom said. "It was a false alarm."

"The baby's fine too," my dad said.

"There's no reason to be sad," they both said.

This made me feel even worse because I hadn't been worried about Mom or the baby. I'd just been worried about myself. My dumb, stupid self.

Because I was the worst person in the world.

I told my parents this, but they didn't believe me,

so I told them everything. About spying on Georgie and sneaking into his room and taking Albert and not giving him back and hiding him in the boys' closet and trying to sneak him over to Georgie's in the middle of the night.

My parents were very quiet while I talked and for many seconds after. "I think we should call Mr. Diaz and Mrs. Tan and explain what happened,"

my dad said. "It doesn't sound to me like you intended to do anything wrong, honey."

"No, you didn't," my mom said, agreeing but not agreeing, because then she said, "But you let yourself get deeper and deeper in trouble when you should have told the truth to begin with. You'll have to apologize. To Georgie and his family."

"Mom!" I cried. "I can't do that! Not to Georgie — I can't talk to Georgie!" First he would yell at me, then he would laugh at me, and then he and Miranda would hang out for the rest of the summer and talk about how much they hated me. The liar, the ferret-stealer, Sylvie Scruggs.

Then my mom told me I had to, and I said I couldn't, and she said I had to, and I said I couldn't, and then she said this wasn't going anywhere, so I said, "All right, fine! Make me do it!" And I sent myself to my room for the rest of my life.

But my room didn't make me feel any better. Everywhere I looked I saw signs of Miranda. Books we'd read together. Dragons we had drawn together.

Barbies we had painted like tigers and cheetahs and leopards together.

When the doorbell rang, I didn't run to the window to see who it was. I just fell on my bed face-first and tried to melt, like a coconut-flavored Popsicle nobody would eat.

There was a tap on my shoulder. I turned my head. Cale's face was right beside mine. "Are you okay?" he said. "You look really sad."

"You look like a squirrel," Tate said.

I sat up to tell them to go away and leave me alone, but I stopped. I couldn't even get mad at my brothers anymore.

"Oh no!" Cale whispered. "Something's really wrong. She can't even talk — give her a hug, Tate."

"No," Tate whispered. "She'll get boogers on my shirt."

"Well, I'm going to hug her," Cale said.

"No, I am," Tate said, and he hugged me so fast he almost missed.

Cale hugged me longer. He patted me on the

shoulder as I sniffed and sniffed. "Don't worry," he said. "They finally caught Albert, and he's fine. Except Georgie said his name was really Dave Thomas, founder of McDonald's, and then he said, 'Did Sylvie really take my ferret?' And we said, 'Yes,' and Georgie said, 'How?' But we didn't know. Then Dad came and got us."

My dad appeared at the door. "There you are, Cale! Your mom would like you and Tate and Sylvie to clean up the ferret mess in your closet — it's not smelling too good. And Sylvie, she says you have one more hour to apologize before I have to take you over there myself. We've explained to Mrs. Tan and Mr. Diaz what happened. All you need to do is say you're sorry."

I let out a sob.

"And also, sweetheart, Miranda is here. She's waiting downstairs."

"No!" I said so fast that Cale jumped away in surprise. "I can't see her, Dad. Tell her I'm sick. Tell her I'm —"

Miranda appeared behind my dad. He turned and smiled like he was glad she was coming over to tell me good-bye forever. "You can tell her whatever you want now, Sylvie." He winked. "Come on, boys. Let's leave them alone."

Dads should never wink.

Miranda walked into the room. "They're making you apologize to Georgie, huh?"

I didn't say anything. I just walked over to my window and looked out at our big maple tree standing a few feet away. Maybe I could jump to the

nearest branch and make my escape before Miranda said "I never want to be your best friend ever again for the rest of my life."

"Thanks for my castle," Miranda said. "It'll be the perfect laboratory. I've already thrown away my old one."

"Oh," I said, still looking out the window.

She took a few steps closer. "Are you still sad?"

"No," I said. "I'm just not feeling good." If she thought I was sick, maybe she'd go away, and I'd never have to hear her say those words, though I would know why she never called and why she wouldn't walk to school with me and why I didn't have any friends.

"You look okay to me," she said. "Except your eyes are kind of red. And your cheeks are all splotchy. But I don't think you have malaria or spotted fever."

"Oh," I said.

"I've missed you," she said when I didn't say anything else.

"Missed me?" I said.

"You're being really dumb," she said.

My chin dropped. Miranda didn't say things like that. She never called me dumb; she was always nice.

"You are," she insisted. "Are you mad at me?"

"Mad at you?" I said. "I'm not mad at you! You're mad at me!"

"No, I'm not," Miranda said, without even blinking.

"But —" I tried to think of all the reasons why she didn't want to be my friend. "I stole Georgie's ferret, and I didn't tell anyone where he was. And I pretended to look for him."

Miranda tilted her head like she was waiting for more.

"And Georgie gave you a microscope, and I just gave you a castle made from blocks. Plus I ruined your birthday party!"

Miranda laughed then. Right at me. "You didn't ruin my birthday party. You know I always expect

the unexpected. And my mom told me what happened at Georgie's. I know you didn't mean to
steal Dave."

I stopped snuffling.

"What you did was pretty dumb," Miranda said.
"But I do dumb things too — remember when I
started our kitchen on fire when we toasted those
earthworms?"

"Oh yeah," I said. "That was kind of dumb."

"And you told me not to," she said. "You thought
it might blow the toaster up. And then there was
that time we were practicing pitching and I threw
the baseball right at your eye socket and it made
you so sick you threw up on my bed. Remember that?"

"Oh yeah," I said. "That hurt. And was gross."

"And remember that rope swing? The one down
in the gully, by the park?"

"Of course," I said, because that happened only a
few months ago. "I told you that rope swing looked
rotten, but you swung on it anyway because you

wanted to measure wind patterns. Then you fell into the gully and got poison oak."

"See!" she said. "We've done lots of stupid things together." She paused and tilted her head, her thinking pose. "We should make a list of every dumb thing we've ever done together. We could record the dates and write down the facts, like where we were and what we damaged. We could draw pictures of what happened since we don't have photos."

I was pretty sure I didn't want to write anything about stealing Albert and ruining Miranda's birthday party. I was pretty sure I wanted to forget what had happened. Forever. But I nodded and smiled, because we had done stupid things together. Lots of them. We were kind of twins that way.

Miranda headed for the door. "You'd better go apologize," she said. "Before your mom gets too mad."

"But wait," I said. She stopped and I looked her right in the face. "You still want to be my friend? Really, really, really?"

"Really," Miranda said. "You're my best friend, and my mom said you can come over later tonight for dinner and we can play castle after."

Everything inside me went all light and fuzzy, because Miranda had said it. She'd said the words out loud. She was still my friend. My best friend.

But I still had to apologize. "I want to come over tonight, but will you come with me to Georgie's now? Please?" Georgie might be nicer to me if Miranda was there.

"I can't," Miranda said. "I have to go to my aunt's house for tea. Why?"

"Because Georgie's your friend," I said. "I don't want to go over there by myself."

But Miranda already had one foot out the door. "He's your friend too," she said, and then she was gone.

Chapter 14

Georgie's humongous dad answered the door.

"Hello," he said, like he'd been expecting me. "Sylvie, right? Please, come in."

I did not come in. I opened my mouth and waited for the words I'd practiced in my bedroom to come out: "I'm so sorry that I took Georgie's ferret. I didn't plan on doing it, but I know that doesn't make it okay. I hope you can forgive me."

"Are you okay?" Georgie's dad said when no words came out.

I nodded. Then I shook my head.

"Your mother called and said you would be coming over to apologize." Georgie's dad seemed to be smiling, but it was hard to tell on his huge, wrinkly face. He backed away from the door, giving me room to get by. "Georgie's in his room. Go ahead and go in."

"I'm sorry," I whispered as I dashed by, heading straight for Georgie's room.

"Hey, Scruggs," Georgie said when he saw me at the door. To my ginormous surprise, Georgie's room was clean today, and he was sitting on his bed reading a book. Albert and the white ferret, the one I'd named Elizabeth, were lying beside him, wrapped up together like a ferret doughnut. They were both asleep.

"I'm sorry for taking Dave," I said.

Georgie put his book down. "This is Roosterfish," he said, pointing to the white ferret. "But we call her Rooster. She's the most glad he's back." He looked straight at my face. "So how did you do it?"

I looked at the clean carpet and realized for the first time that it was blue. "I'm sorry" was all I said.

Georgie stood up and came closer. "My dad said you came in through the window, but how, exactly? The windows are pretty high and my grandma always locks them. Did you use a credit card to break it open? I tried a credit card in a door once, but it snapped in half."

"Credit cards only work on little doors," I explained, because I had once done a credit-card-opening experiment too.

Then I told him exactly how I got in his room, and he told me all the ways he'd tried to break

in to his house just for fun. Or in case there was a fire and he had to rescue his grandma. Or his ferrets.

"I never thought of that," I said, because if a fire happened at my house, I'd have to rescue the new baby and the twins. So we talked for a while about breaking in to houses in the middle of a fire or a robbery or a murder, and all of a sudden, it was time to leave.

"Want to play some ball tomorrow?" Georgie said. "Down at the park?"

"Sure," I said with a shrug. "Miranda and I can walk over together."

"Miranda?" Georgie said with a "Huh?" kind of face. Then he shrugged. "I thought she didn't play baseball. But I guess that's all right. She can come too."

The next day, Josh, Georgie, Miranda, and I were at the baseball diamond with some of Georgie's baseball friends. Georgie split us up into two teams, and I was not on Georgie's team.

Then he told the guys on my side that I should pitch. They nodded, like they'd been expecting this, but I was suspicious. Georgie probably thought his team would win if I pitched.

Georgie was first up to bat.

Luckily, my ankle was pretty much better. *You can do it this time,* I told myself as I stepped onto the pitcher's mound. *You can beat the pants off him. Strike him out.*

"Come on, Scruggs," Georgie said as he stood at home plate. He swung the bat back and forth in front of him. "Let's see what ya got. Not much in the way of pow-a, I'd say."

Nobody laughed at this, and a few of the guys on my team groaned like Georgie said that joke all the time, so I straddled the pitcher's mound as if his words didn't bother me. In one smooth motion, I pulled my legs together, the ball and glove coming up to my chest. "You'd better close your eyes," I told

Georgie. "Or this throw's going to make them both fall out."

Then I raised my arms up over my head and threw. The ball soared out of my hand, zooming in a perfect line toward the plate.

Georgie's eyeballs fell out. Okay, they didn't really fall out, but they almost did. He swung with all his strength —

And missed.

"Strike!" Josh called, even though he was on Georgie's team.

Georgie dug his bat into the ground. He scratched his head. Then he said something I thought he would never, ever say. "Nice pitch, Scruggs."

"Go, Sylvie!" Miranda cried. She was standing by the fence with the rest of Georgie's team, last in the lineup. "Great pitch!"

"She's not on our team," one of the boys said to her.

"I know," Miranda said. "But I can still cheer for her, right? You can cheer for both sides."

I looked at Josh, next up to bat. He shrugged. I looked at Georgie, who was already cocking up his bat for a second try. I looked at the other guys on the field, who were really pretty nice, for boys. They were mostly scratching their armpits.

I looked at Miranda and smiled so big you could probably see lots of my teeth. "You can cheer for everybody," I said.

Acknowledgments

Sylvie would still be fishing Muffin out of a gold-fish pool if it weren't for the help of my family and friends.

My particular thanks go to the people at the Vermont College of Fine Arts (the best MFA writing program in the universe, as Sylvie would say). Martine Leavitt, Leda Schubert, Tim Wynne-Jones, Shelley Tanaka, and Margaret Bechard, my glorious advisors, your wisdom will forever be in my head.

Thank you to my dear friends who read multiple (multiple!) versions of this book: Skila Brown, Erin Hagar, Maggie Lehrman, Stefanie Lyons, Kristin Sandoval, Amy Zinn, and Quinn Silcox.

To my extended family on both sides — thank you for your constant, fervent support.

Tremendous thanks go to Caitlin Blasdell, my wise and tenacious agent, and Cheryl Klein, my gifted and careful editor. Thank you for loving Sylvie and reining her in when her antics spin out of control!

Mary, Lucy, Calvin, Shaemus, and Flannery — thank you for listening to version after version of this book. Thank you for loving to read, thank you for being the best kids a mother could have, and thank you for loving me.

Thank you, Sam, for being my best friend, my biggest cheerleader, and my number-one best reader/advisor/suggestion-giver ever (the baseball bit was your idea!). You are my Georgie (and that is a very good thing).

And most important, thank you to my Father in Heaven for guidance, patience, and this wonderful chance at life.

ABOUT THE AUTHOR

Lindsay Eyre is a mother of five, a graduate of the MFA program in Creative Writing at the Vermont College of Fine Arts, and a fanatical lover of books. *The Best Friend Battle* is her debut novel. She lives in the grand but sweaty city of Cary, North Carolina. Please visit her website at www.lindsayeyre.com and follow her at @lindsayeyre.

ABOUT THE ILLUSTRATOR

Charles Santoso is a concept artist and illustrator who loves to draw very little things in a very little journal. He currently resides in Sydney, Australia. Please visit his website at www.charlessantoso.com and follow him at @minitreehouse.

This book was edited by Cheryl Klein and designed by Jeannine Riske. The production was supervised by Elizabeth Starr Baer. The text was set in Bembo, with display type set in Futura. This book was printed and bound by R. R. Donnelley in Crawfordsville, Indiana. The manufacturing was supervised by Shannon Rice.